'HOOD VIBRATIONS

A Law of Attraction Story for Teens

Ann Benton

BALBOA.
PRESS

A DIVISION OF HAY HOUSE

Balboa Press books may be ordered through booksellers or by contacting:

Balboa Press
A Division of Hay House
1663 Liberty Drive
Bloomington, IN 47403
www.balboapress.com
1-(877) 407-4847

ISBN: 978-1-4525-0078-2 (sc)
ISBN: 978-1-4525-0106-2 (e)

Library of Congress Control Number: 2010915751

Printed in the United States of America

Balboa Press rev. date: 11/17/2010

"Whether you think you can or you think you can't,
either way you are right."
Henry Ford (1863-1947)

~ INTRODUCTION ~

I first heard about the Law of Attraction in May of 2008. It was at the perfect time in my life. I had just separated from my husband of 13 years, had a 12-year-old daughter to raise by myself, and a very small income to support us. I did not know how we were going to make it financially. From my perspective, nothing I had done previously in my life had worked out very well - from unhealthy relationships, to lack of money, to health problems. I had always looked outside myself for answers to my difficulties, and was always disappointed. So, I was ready and willing to make some very different choices in every area of my life.

Only one week after my husband left and I was feeling sad and alone, one of my grown sons who has two daughters of his own, sent me a copy of Rhonda Byrne's "The Secret" DVD. I watched it the minute it arrived, and my life changed that day!

As a visualization technique in the movie, Mike Dooley, author of *Infinite Possibilities: The Art of Living Your Dreams* and one of the teachers of The Secret, suggested looking at the back of your hands, with the freckles, wrinkles, rings, and nails, and then picturing your fingers wrapped around the steering wheel of your new car. I didn't need a car, so I visualized the nasty skin cancer which had been growing on my hand for six months being totally healed before my appointment with the dermatologist in three weeks. Every day, I pictured my hand looking as healthy as before. My husband and daughter witnessed the total and complete healing of that spot within three weeks. By the time I went to my appointment to have it removed, the doctor couldn't even tell it had been there!

After that, I studied everything I could watch, listen to and read about the Law of Attraction. Like Jack Canfield, author of the *Chicken Soup for the Soul* book series and one of the teachers of The Secret, I changed a $10 bill into a $100,000 bill with a magic marker and pasted it on my "vision board."

Every day, I pictured the kind of lifestyle I would be living with that kind of money. More importantly, I believed it was coming to me. Absolutely.

Three months later, I received a settlement from a legal case which had slipped through the cracks for the past four years. It settled suddenly, and for what amount? $100,000!

I became obsessed with learning all I could about this new-to-me secret, reading books and listening to audio recordings by Law of Attraction teachers like: Esther and Jerry Hicks, Bob Proctor, John Assaraf, T. Harv Eker, Lisa Nichols, Michael Beckwith, Bob Doyle, Wayne

Dyer, Earl Nightengale, Louise Hay, Susan Jeffers, Eckhart Tolle, John Randolph Price, Byron Katie, and many more. I subscribed to dozens of internet resources, such as newsletters and daily motivational messages. I discovered there was so much free sharing and abundance for all!

I read Joe Vitale's *The Attractor Factor* and began to ask the Universe for a money-making idea. I did not want another dead-end office job. In his book, Joe advised to "dare something worthy" of your life. I needed an idea that would "scare me a little and excite me a lot."

Soon, the Universe delivered an idea I never would have thought of myself. It was big, and exciting, and scary, and I knew immediately this was it!

What if children could be taught the Law of Attraction *before* they learned all the self-limiting beliefs that our culture instilled in them – while they still believed they could do, be, or have anything?

Imagine their potential, their fulfillment, and their impact on the world! "I'll write a children's book about this," I thought. That really made me excited and scared and certainly fit the description of doing something that was worthy of my life.

I looked online to see if anyone else had thought of this before me. I found some great websites and several children's books on the subject. Mostly, though, I found lots of how-parents-can-teach-kids kinds of books. There were very few aimed directly at young readers illustrating how they could apply the Law of Attraction themselves.

So I set to work on the first of what I envision as a series of books for teens and pre-teens, harnessing the great power of story to hold kids' attention and aid them in understanding the principles being revealed.

Then – as though to validate my own efforts – *The Secret to Teen Power* by Paul Harrington, producer of "The Secret" DVD, came out the fall of '09.

I was so excited, I ran out and bought two copies the day it was released! This was a wonderful book and easier for me to read than most of the adult books on the subject. Paul's book explained the Law of Attraction in teen lingo and was a great introduction and prelude to my own book series.

Again, though, the book was a nonfiction, how-to book. As I said, I elected to take a different tack on teaching the Law of Attraction to young folks – a series of stories that illustrate real-life applications of the Law of Attraction in kids' lives.

At that time, I had not yet run across Liliane Grace's *The Mastery Club*. She has written the perfect Law of Attraction novel for teens and pre-teens!

What a great way to mesh all these approaches to educate and inspire our kids to create their joy-filled lives earlier than most of us!

Today's youth learned how to recycle before some of us had even heard of separating trash; to communicate technologically on Google, Twitter and Facebook, when some of us were still trying to think up an email password; to ignore racial, religious, economic, and sexual-orientation differences some of us didn't think we would see happen in our lifetimes!

The timing is perfect. People like you and me are raising consciousness all over the world.

When beliefs in lack and limitation end; when everyone knows their power and potential for joy and abundance, then we will have world peace. It starts with each of us ... here and now. All we have to do is believe in our dreams, let go of "conventional wisdom," and embrace the Power Within.

So without further ado, allow me introduce you to 'HOOD VIBRATIONS: A LAW OF ATTRACTION STORY FOR TEENS, the first book in the series.

'HOOD VIBRATIONS is about a boy who uses the Law of Attraction to change his life from living in the poverty of the ghetto to living in a world of prosperity and possibilities, limited only by his imagination.

The second and third books in the series illustrate how two more young folks use the Law of Attraction to improve their health and relationships. These stories are written for young folks (12 and older) in age-appropriate language. They are books kids can read for themselves.

You were attracted to this book for a reason. Now take inspired action! Read the story, try the experiments for yourself, and reap the rewards of your "good vibrations." Couldn't be easier! Enjoy, and tell me what you think.

You can contact me at: www.LawOfAttractionJr. com. Visit me here and learn how I recently used the Law of Attraction to manifest the car of my dreams!

Good vibrations to all! ~Ann

CHAPTER ONE –
"THE DRIVE-BY"

Though it is bright out under the streetlight, from where Silas Brown watches from deep in the shadows of the abandoned warehouse, he is invisible. Second Avenue is like that as it runs through the inner city – a nest of abandoned buildings and homes, many of them pressed into service as crack houses. Their own gang house, two blocks over on West Fourth, is just such a place.

Silas is the lookout for the gang, the Southside Seminoles, and it is an important job. Earlier that evening, their leader, Madrid, told him, "Look alive, boy. You got our backs. Don't want nothin' to catch us blindside. Be hell to pay, hear me? Keep yo' peepers peeled."

There is an abandoned furniture factory across the street, and their gang graffiti covers much of the red-brick wall. The artwork, most of it in their gang colors of burgundy and tan, is a mural of one and two-fingered hand signs and handguns; of the faces of gang leaders and important events in gang history, like the gunfight

1

with the Saracens in Southside Park last year. That cost them three of their best brothers. The image of their former leader and founder, Bandy, stares out through prison bars.

Some of the art is so fresh, the paint glistens under the streetlight.

Fresher still, though, are the gray dots of nine-millimeter, machine gun fire that deface Madrid's handiwork. There would be hell to pay for that – payback for the diss, the disrespect, for the violation of their turf.

Silas shivers and looks fearfully behind him. Lookout is also a dangerous job as any number of people, mostly his family and friends, told him. People like his mother, who knows what he is doing and alternately cries and threatens him. She calls him names, "stupid boy," and reminds him of what happened to his cousin, Maurice, on the other side of town.

Maurice took a bullet in the spine and lives in a wheelchair now. Once the best point guard at Martin Luther King Middle School, these days Maurice plays basketball for the Paralympics, and wears a diaper in case – in the excitement of a fast break – he pees his pants.

But thinking of his mother shames Silas. He is supposed to be a man now. Though he is only twelve, he was given a man's job to do.

The squeal of tires brings him out of his daydream – the shriek of a car cornering too fast. It gives way to the roar of a racing engine. But the sound is far away, far down Second Avenue. He listens hard, listens till his ears chirp, but does not hear it again. He hears only the thump, the bass line, of a rap song coming from an apartment in the projects two blocks over.

After a moment, Silas takes a step out onto the sidewalk and looks down the dark street. He stares into the darkness till his eyes tear up. But the way is clear as far as he can see. Just purplish pools of streetlight at each intersection.

Silas is still in the open when the shot comes. He sees the flash in the black box of a broken window across the street. There is the shock like being punched. He is down on his back before he knows it.

He touches his shoulder and his hand comes away wet. Under the streetlight, the blood looks almost black.

I'm shot, he thinks, not believing it. I've been shot.

Gunfire is returned, raking the building. It is answered by more of the same from the black hole of the window.

A yell comes from inside the building, and the gunfire stops.

Still on his back, Silas hears the sound of sneaker-shod feet running toward him, squeaking, and suddenly the whole gang is over him, blocking the streetlights.

Someone, Jermaine, is on the cell phone calling it in. "Yeh, I wanna report a shootin'. Second Avenue at the old furniture factory. Yeh, somebody shot. Be a bro'. Bleedin' bad. Get here quick!"

And now Madrid is over him. He has a white tee shirt and he presses it to Silas's shoulder. As he does, the pain rocks him.

"Hold it there, Silas." he tells him. "Press it tight! Ambulance comin'."

And right on cue, Silas hears a siren, still faraway, but closing fast, louder, echoing down the canyon of brick and concrete.

When it is just a block away, the gang stands.

"Gotta go," Madrid tells him, looking down. "Be a three-time loser if they catch me here. You took one for us, Silas. Won't forget it."

With that, they are gone, shoes squeaking. Silas turns to look after them, and the motion brings another wave of pain. With a groan, he passes out.

Being lifted wakes him. He finds himself on a gurney, a stretcher with wheels. There are two paramedics working over him, a man and a woman. The lights of the ambulance and the police cars bathe everything in red and blue, so that the two look strange, alien to Silas.

A uniformed cop with a notebook is asking him something. Silas can't hear him – because his mother is there now, and she is crying. His big sister, Latisha, is crying too. Both the twins are upset and crying.

Silas feels himself being rolled, then lifted again into the ambulance. His view is dominated by shelves with red crosses on them and a machine with a little TV screen.

The woman paramedic gets in beside him. She has blood on her white shirt. The man slams the back door and a moment later, Silas hears the driver's door open and slam.

Almost instantly, the engine fires and the ambulance begins to move.

As they rock over the curb and into the street, the siren starts above him.

The woman paramedic is kneeling beside the gurney, and there is a sharp prick in the crook of his elbow as she starts an IV. Then another prick in his arm near his shoulder and Silas is asleep.

CHAPTER TWO –
"CITY HOSPITAL"

Silas awakens on the operating room table. He looks up at the big round light above him. It looks like a silvery moon. The doctors and nurses are gathered around, wearing blue gowns and caps with blue masks over their faces.

A face blocks the light. A man's face.

"Hey, Silas, I'm Dr. Morgan. I want you to relax, okay? You're going to be fine. I'm from the 'hood, too, so bullets are my specialty. I see a lot of kids from Second Avenue come through here." After a moment, he smiles. "I guess you're not fast enough to get out the way of a bullet, eh? Never make it as a pro."

Silas smiles. The drugs are making him woozy and the pain is gone.

"Well," Dr. Morgan tells him. "Here we go. Sweet dreams. See you on the flip-side."

He looks over at another one of the doctors and nods. Silas is looking at the light above him, when suddenly, it explodes in shards of silver glass, and the world goes black.

In what seems like a second later, Silas wakes up in his hospital room. It is daytime. Through the window across the room, he sees blue sky over a yellow-brick building. City pigeons sail by, squawking. The window is open, and clown-print curtains stir in the breeze.

"Silas? Honey, you 'wake?"

His mother is sitting in the chair beside his bed. Her bible rests in her lap. She peers at him over the half-moon reading glasses perched on the end of her nose. She looks so comical in the glasses that Silas smiles. He is also warmed by this familiar touch of home. Even with the windows open, the room has a clinical smell.

"How you feelin'?"

"Okay, I guess. Thirsty."

From a side-table, his mother pours a glass of water and hands it to him. (The glass has the same clowns on it as the curtains.) Silas's right arm is in a sling, and when he reaches for the water with that hand, the pain in his shoulder is so great, he feels faint. He settles back on the pillows with a groan.

"Oh, baby," his mother says. "Let me hold it for you."

The water is ice cold and about the best thing Silas has ever tasted.

"Slow down, Sugar. Not so fast," his mom cautions.

When he finally stops, the straw is making rude noises in the bottom of the clown glass.

"Where is everybody?"

7

"Home. Working. Missus Porter is watching the twins." Mrs. Porter is their neighbor across the hall. "Latisha will be by later. Said she'd bring you a sandwich." She nods toward a plate on the nightstand. "Food here is terrible!"

"Knock-knock."

They look up. It's Doctor Morgan. "Just checking on you. You look pretty good, considering. Are you hungry yet?" he asks Silas.

"Not really."

"Well, you will be by this afternoon. If you behave, I'll order something for you. What would you like? A cup of soup?"

"You kidding? How 'bout a cheeseburger?"

"A gut bomb?"

"And large fries," Silas grins.

"We'll see. Food service here ought to be shot. Oops! Guess that's no laughing matter hereabouts."

But, in fact, all three of them are laughing.

CHAPTER THREE – "BACK TO SCHOOL"

"Yo, Silas, what happened this time?"

Rudy, Silas's good friend from Elmwood, comes up to him in the schoolyard that first day of the new school year. Rudy doesn't live in Silas's neighborhood. He waits excitedly till school starts each fall for a blow-by-blow of Silas's gang exploits. It is safer to live vicariously off Silas – as the sling on his right arm clearly proves.

"Oughta see the other guy," Silas says with a smile.

"No doubt. He has slings on *both* arms."

"And two broken legs."

"Not to mention a broken nose."

Now the friends slap hands and hug.

"Good to see you, man."

"Same-same."

Silas pulls out a cigarette from his shirt pocket and offers one to Rudy. "God sakes, Silas. You're *twelve*!" Rudy responds, rolling disapproving eyes.

It has been a bad summer for Silas – but really pretty much true to form – and after all, he has survived. He survived! The school year began just two weeks after his hospital stay. His arm, still in a cast, is now heavily autographed. Madrid had come by his house when his mom wasn't home and drew a picture of Silas holding crossed nine-millimeter handguns. For the better part of a week, Silas was able to hide Madrid's artwork from his mother. When she finally saw it – one night as she was scratching the itch in his healing wound – she turned the guns into crosses with a black magic marker.

Other gang bangers had left their handiwork, too - but really no one could draw like Madrid. His guns looked real enough to load and shoot.

It has always been tough in the 'hood. Silas's dad took off right after the twins were born – just up and abandoned them all. Wanted his freedom. Silas was very angry. Still is. His mom was overloaded with two jobs and four kids. The money and food stamps they received from welfare helped some, but even after Latisha was old enough to go to work, her minimum wage job still wasn't enough. As a result, Silas's mother was stressed out and cranky all the time – always worried about money.

Silas tried to help out the only way he could – by running deliveries and being lookout for the gang. For that, he scored a little folding money once in a while. But his mother knew where it came from, and it just gave her more to worry about.

Worst of all, a gang held its turf with violence or the threat of it. Silas was always there, always at the center of any throw-down. He wanted so much to be a tough guy – the man of the house - to fill the void his absentee father had left in all their lives.

The school bell rings as Silas finishes catching Rudy up on his exciting summer. Silas takes a final drag and flicks the cig toward the netless hoop hanging from the side of the building. It goes through – perhaps, Silas hopes, a good omen.

"Two points," says Rudy.

"*Three* points," says Silas.

CHAPTER FOUR – "DETENTION"

Silas's age group is in seventh grade now, but because of his poor performance and attendance record, he is repeating the sixth grade. All his teachers tell him he is smart, but his grades keep slipping more and more each year.

Silas ends up with all the same teachers as last year, with one exception. A new science teacher, Mr. Barnes, is taking over the sixth grade class while Mrs. Jackson is out with another new baby. As Silas takes his seat on the first day of class, he observes that Mr. Barnes appears to be from the "upper" side of town. He's black, but dresses like a white preppie – khaki pants, buttoned-down collar, and a green pullover sweater. "This guy's gonna catch all kinda bad around here," Silas thinks to himself. "We gonna have some fun with him."

Negative attention is better than no attention, Silas has learned. He ends up in after-school detention before the first week of school is over, on multiple counts – disrupting class, cheating, not turning in homework, smoking on school grounds, bullying, and fighting.

His father told Silas before he left that he would "never amount to no good." Silas seems out to prove him right.

Silas arrives 10 minutes late to his first detention session. He figures he is in as much trouble as he can be anyway. Sitting in detention is a waste of time. Always has been.

"I was just about to take attendance," comes a voice from the front of the room. "Glad you made it in time." It is Mr. Barnes speaking. The new teacher always gets detention duty. There are only four students in detention that first week. As Mr. Barnes approaches Silas's desk, he tells the class that he wants to have a little one-on-one time with each student. "Yeh, startin' with the 'no dang good' kid," Silas thinks to himself. "What does uptight, button-down-man Barnes want?" Truth is, Mr. Barnes sees himself in the kid.

"I hear you live on Kennedy Street."

"Yeh."

"I grew up on Tuskegee. Just one block over. I was a Saracen."

Silas gives the teacher a skeptical look. He glances at the alligator logo. He may have grown up on the street, Silas thinks. But he's a long way from it now. Like a million miles.

Mr. Barnes sees where Silas is looking. He plucks at the Izod logo.

"This? The badge of success, Silas. It took me a long time to earn it. Never would have if I didn't get some help. Somebody who showed me how to turn my life around by turning my thinking around."

"Huh?"

"Mind if I sit with you?"

"Suit yourself." Silas wonders why grownups are so stupid.

"I was just like you at your age. Into the same things - belonged to a gang, spent my nights breaking into houses, lifting stereos out of cars, fighting. Not much different at home. My dad beat up on my mom every time he got drunk – which was whenever he could afford it. Paydays mostly. Which left the family without food and close to being homeless most months."

"Yeh," Silas tells him. "Been there, done that." "What *is* this," Silas wonders, "true confessions?"

"I bet. Twice the cops picked me up – but I got out of it because of my age. I was only twelve at the time."

"How'd you get here?"

"A teacher."

Silas rolls his eyes. "Sure."

"That's right. A science teacher. A Mr. Holmes, to be exact. He taught me about the power of my thinking – my thinking mind - to create a life of abundance; that I have the power to attract positive instead of negative people and circumstances into my own life."

Silas snorts and hums the theme from the "Twilight Zone."

"I'm serious."

Silas groans. "My mind? My thinking mind?" Silas says, mimicking Mr. Barnes. "That's so *not* cool."

"Okay. Would you rather be cool or happy?"

"Rather be rich. Then I'd be cool *and* happy."

"Silas, how are you going to get rich in the 'hood? I know what it's like here. What you're more likely to get is *dead*!"

"Man, I'm teflon," Silas mutters as he leans back in his chair.

"If Mr. Holmes hadn't come along, I know exactly where I'd be right now – pushing up daisies. I came back here to give kids like you and the other students over there what Mr. H. gave me – a way out of the 'hood.

"Okay, okay." Silas resigns himself to listening to Mr. Barnes's sermon whether he wants to or not. Nothin' else to do.

"Mr. Holmes treated me with respect. For the first time in my life, I began to trust someone. He set boundaries, held me accountable for my actions and attitudes, and enforced *fair* consequences.

I remember one time … I talked my best friend, Tony, into skipping school with me and taking Mr. Holmes's car for a 'joy ride.' Mr. H. had a sweet, red convertible sports car I just *had* to get my hands on. We were only 13 years old and pretty full of ourselves. Anyway, I hot-wired the car and we drove around town smoking cigarettes and blasting the radio as loud as it would go. Man, did she hug the curves! When we got back to school, I parked the car exactly as I had found it. We were back in time for the next class and thought we'd gotten away with our 'crime.' As it turned out, Mr. Holmes let class out a bit early and as he was walking to the parking lot to retrieve his lunch bag out of his car, he spotted us heading for our next class. We might not have looked so suspicious if we had not just skipped his class, and if we'd come back in time for the engine to cool down. Seems Mr. H. had just gotten his car out of the shop that morning and happened to have the odometer reading on his receipt. He became suspicious when he felt the warmth of the engine and checked out the mileage. Sure enough, it had 40 miles more than that morning. And where had we been during class time?"

"You guys were so busted!" Silas chimes in. He surprises himself by being interested in the *joy ride*. The others in detention are drawing cartoons on their notebooks and pretending to look out the window, but Silas can tell by their shifting eyes that they are listening too.

"Yeah, but Mr. Holmes didn't turn us in to the principal or call our parents. Instead, he called a taxi cab company to see what the charge would be to ride 40 miles. It was about $25, which was a lot of bread back then. The next day after class, he had a little chat with us. He talked about choices and responsibility and respect for other people's property. In the end, he expected us to pay him back the amount of money it would have cost to take a 40-mile ride in a cab. You know – money for gas and for wear and tear on his car. He said that little incident would be just between the three of us. Then, he instructed that the money we would pay back had to be earned *legally* and could not come from our families."

"Wow, bummer."

"*And,* Mr. Holmes required that we prove our source of income and show our accounting methods. He said he was confident that we could figure it all out and pay him by the end of three months.

Well, Tony and I didn't have a clue how we'd earn money if it didn't include drug deals and such. But after a while, and with Mr. H's frequent prompting of 'How's the project coming?' we both came up with something. Tony got a newspaper route that he could deliver on his bicycle. I found out that I could make more money selling skateboard parts separately than as a whole, so with the money I made selling the parts (like wheels, brackets, and bearings), I was able to buy another skateboard, break it down and sell its parts. It took a while, but both of us met Mr. Holmes's deadline. Might have been the first honorable thing we'd ever done. We were proud of ourselves and so was Mr. H."

"Hmmm." Silas thinks selling skateboard parts is a pretty cool idea. "How'd you think of that?" he asks Mr. Barnes.

"Good question. One day when Mr. Holmes asked me about 'the project,' I told him that I was getting angry and frustrated at not coming up with an idea yet. He suggested that instead of saying to myself, 'I can't,' that I start saying 'How can I?' Soon after trying his suggestion – BAM – it hit me! I was in business."

Sounds more interesting than a paper route."

"I thought so."

"In time," Mr. Barnes goes on, "I began to want to be like my teacher. Mr. Holmes taught me, by his example, to look for the best in people and situations and when I did, that's what I started getting – the best! You ever experienced that, Silas? Wanting to be like someone with qualities you admire?"

"Nah. Well … my grandpa, I s'pose. He lived next door when I was a kid. Played cards with me. Taught me how to keep a straight poker face. Slipped me a slug of whiskey and a cigarette now and then. Dead now. Shot in a drive-by."

"I'm sorry, Silas. Sounds like he spent some good times with you being your friend. That's a great quality! You have good qualities too, you know?"

"What the…?!!!" Silas lets out a loud yell when he feels a sharp sting on the back of his neck. He and Mr. B. turn quickly and catch the other boys trying to hide their rubberbands and spitballs.

"Knock it off, boys," Mr. Barnes instructs.

"Suck-up. Brown-noser. Butt-kisser." Silas's detention mates whisper under their breaths. They have been amusing themselves, but are getting rowdy.

Mr. Barnes tells them, "Get out a sheet of paper and write 'I have much more potential than shooting spitballs' 100 times."

The boys howl. "Hey Silas, I got me more potential than shooting spitballs," one boy says. "How 'bout you, Si-lass? You Mr. Potential now?" They keep laughing but write their list. Silas knows they all just want to be released when the bell rings.

"Geeez, way to go, dork!" one of the boys mumbles to the shooter.

"So, what is it that you want to be, do, or have?" Mr. Barnes looks back to Silas.

"I want to be the head of a gang with lots of tattoos, knives, a machine gun, a fast car, and plenty of dope."

"Would that make your life happier?"

"I'd be really cool and really powerful!"

"You are powerful now," Barnes tells him. "And when you see what using the power of your mind can do, you'll be cool. Your mind is a powerful magnet. You attract whatever you focus on. You're doing it already!"

"No way." Silas thinks about this. "What do you mean?" he asks.

"Well, what do you think about on a daily basis – like when you get up in the morning?"

"I think about my S.O.B. dad. His leaving me. Saying I'd never amount to no good."

"And how do you feel when you remember that?"

"Pissed."

"Kinda like the world's done you wrong and you've got to fight for everything?"

"Yeh."

"What's your life like right now? Do good things come to you pretty easily? High grades, your safety and physical health, friends that bring out the best in you?"

"Nah, it stinks! Everything's a struggle. Can't do anything right. Nothin's easy."

"Do you see how when you think about not amounting to much, especially when you add feelings like anger to those thoughts, you attract more circumstances that prove you right? What you think about, you bring about. That's not original," remarks Mr. B., "but it works here.

By constantly thinking you're the toughest, meanest 12-year old in school, and fueling that thinking with anger, fear, dishonesty and discontent, you are powerfully creating that exact situation."

"Say what?"

For the first time, a teacher has Silas's undivided attention. Even the other students' cutting up and snickering do not distract him now.

"Silas, if you want something better, you first have to create the picture of what you want in your mind."

"Picture in my mind? Like a home entertainment wall-to-wall picture screen?" Silas retorts sarcastically.

"Here's a short science lesson," Mr. Barnes instructs. "All of creation is made up of particles of energy which vibrate at a certain frequency. A universal law called the Law of Attraction says that by focusing your thinking on the thing you want most – let's say, a gold watch – you are tuning the frequency of your mind energy to the frequency of the watch you have imagined – like tuning in a radio to a certain station – and you will attract it because like attracts like."

"No way."

"Yes, way. When you focus on what you want, it's called *visualizing*. It's like fantasizing or daydreaming. The laws of the universe are always working – just like the Law of Gravity – and always listening to your thoughts. Like I said before, if you think negative thoughts and feel negative emotions all the time – like fear and anger –

you'll attract more situations that give you more negative thoughts and emotions."

"Really?"

"Yeah, really. You'll know they're negative by the way they feel in your body. How does your gut feel when you think of your father?"

"Ow! Knots! Hard to breathe. He done my mom wrong. Done us all wrong!"

"Yes, why do you think he did that?"

"He's stupid." Silas remembers how it feels when he is called the same thing. "Well, maybe, he ... you know, didn't know better either, like me."

"Maybe. How do you know if something is better?"

Silas shrugs.

"You'll know your thoughts and emotions are positive if you feel calm and peaceful in your body - like the good feelings you get when you're helping out a friend. Can you feel that?"

"Yeh." Silas nods. When he and Rudy catch up every fall, it feels easy.

"The best part is that if you think positive thoughts and feel positive emotions, you will attract more situations that give you more positive thoughts and emotions. It's the Law."

"You kiddin' me? I ain't always been big on the law."

"Trust me - you will on this one."

The bell rings and detention is finally over for the day. The other students escape to freedom with their cartoons, books, and spitball supplies.

Silas leaves quietly. He is thinking. "What's all that stuff Mr. B. said? Pretty weird." When he gets outside, he lights up a smoke and walks through the littered alley all the way to the gang house – only this time, a bit more slowly than usual.

CHAPTER FIVE – "THE ASSIGNMENT"

Of course, it takes Silas a while to absorb the things his teacher has told him. His thinking has become so ingrained, it is hard to find a new point of view. But by the time his next detention session rolls around, he is ready to hear more about this Law of Attraction thing that will make him the most powerful guy on Second Avenue. He asks Mr. Barnes how to do it.

"Tell you what - I'm going to give you an assignment. I want you to try it out for yourself for the next couple of weeks. You'll need a few more details, though, to make this work. First, don't think of what you don't want. Your subconscious mind does not recognize 'don't, not, and no.' It just gives you what you think about. Okay?"

"Huh? Sounds confusin'."

"First, focus on what you want. Visualize it in detail. What do you want, Silas?"

"I want a skateboard."

"Good. What color?"

"Black with red lightning bolts painted on top."

"Even better. By visualizing or imagining the thing you want, you are putting yourself on the same vibrational frequency as what you want to attract. Believe that it is possible for you to have the thing you want. Unbelief attracts more unbelief."

"Vibrational frequency? For real?"

"Yes. Now picture yourself riding on your new skateboard. How does it feel?"

"It feels kinda cool and fun. I want to jump curbs with it."

"Great! See yourself jumping curbs. That's the most important part. You must *feel* the feelings, the excitement and joy that you would feel if you already had the thing you want. Feelings are what add power to your attraction. Still with me?"

"I guess."

"Then, let your request go out into the universe and sincerely express your gratitude that your mind's desire is now on its way. Using this method puts your mind vibrations on a matching frequency with the thing you desire."

"What about matching my frequency to some bling? You know... to the vibration of cash?"

"Well, sure. Everyone wants cash, but I don't mean to imply that whatever you want just falls out of the sky. Reaching our goals requires taking some action.

"Figures."

"When I was your age, I wanted lots of money too. Mr. Holmes advised me to get my education first. Knowledge is power. It yields money. So I got through school and became a successful lawyer, a very RICH, successful lawyer."

"How'd you make that law-thing work for you?"

"Well, everyday I imagined myself bringing home my report card, feeling excited to tell my mother about my big turnaround from D's to B's. Next, I saw myself at graduation, celebrating, happy, proud, my mom crying tears of joy. I did the same thing through college. Then I held a vision of myself at my desk at work, in a corner office overlooking the city, wearing expensive suits and earning tons of money. As it turned out, I made more money than I could ever spend. I work at Martin Luther King Middle School now just to teach kids that there is a way out of the 'hood. Kids like you, Silas."

Silas folds his arms. "Sounds too easy," he tells him.

"I thought so, too. At first. Until I tried it. Then I attracted a bicycle I'd always wanted. And within 30 days!"

"No lie?"

"Absolutely. I began to consciously choose better thoughts in order to attract more good stuff. And when I chose to drop the angry, negative attitudes and behaviors, I started getting along better with my family, friends and teachers."

"Teachers are stupid. Oh, sorry Mr. B."

"If that's what you think about them, that's what you'll get more of."

"My mind's really that powerful?"

"No doubt about it! You create your own happiness or your own suffering. Are you ready to try that homework assignment now?"

"Well, ok."

The bell rings but the other students in detention hang back a little. Were they listening?

"Do you get all that stuff?" they ask Silas. Silas tries to translate it as they slowly go down the hall. He notices that, like him, each of them seems absorbed in their own thoughts.

CHAPTER SIX – "PROGRESS"

Two weeks later, Silas and Mr. Barnes run into each other in the lunchroom at school.

"How did your experiment with the Law of Attraction go, Silas?"

"Well, I did try to think about a way to make money without getting shot! I pictured myself with pockets full of money, wearin' this cool-looking gold chain I saw in a storefront window, ridin' around in a nice car, movin' into a new house – out of the 'hood. You know, tryin' to get the right *vibes* goin'. After a couple days of focusin' on this stuff, I walked by ole man Henry's Food Mart on First Street after leavin' the gang house. He stops me and says he could use some help. One of his guys didn't show up for work again. He had more shelves to stock than he could handle. Said he'd pay me. Somethin' told me to go ahead, so I gave him a couple hours. No sweat. He did pay – with cash and food. Said he'd like me to come back the next day too."

"Good, Silas. Good." Mr. B. was listening intently.

"I brought the food home to my mom and kept the money for my smokes. Then, I started thinkin' I'd have more money if I didn't smoke. Started imaginin' more dough in my pocket, and I did it – I quit!"

"Wow! Great, Silas!"

"That money's already startin' to add up. I like a full stomach and full pockets. Now, I'm workin' at Henry's store every afternoon. Leaves me short on time with my homies though. I catch a lot of heat for that, but I really wanna prove my dad wrong."

"Very good, Silas. You listened well," replied Mr. Barnes. "Sounds like you got a feel for how the Law of Attraction works. Stay positive, expect the best, take action toward your dreams, and your life will keep getting better. And don't forget gratitude for what you have now. But keep dreaming big, and bigger."

"Yeh, was kinda fun."

"Now that you have a steady stream of income, how about trying the Law of Attraction on your school work? Mid-terms are coming up in three weeks, you know."

"I guess I could give it a 'shot' – pun intended," Silas says with a grin.

CHAPTER SEVEN –
"THE RESULTS"

Silas manages to stay out of detention for the next three weeks. And despite catching flack from his gang brothers, he becomes better friends with Rudy, the nerdy guy from Elmwood. Rudy has a good influence on Silas. He is a fairly good student, is respectful of others, and keeps things light.

It has been a grueling mid-term week for Silas and his last exam is in science. He has never been good at taking tests and now he is the last one to finish. As he is turning his paper in, Mr. Barnes asks him to stay for a few minutes after class. Says he wants to talk to him.

"How did your experiment with the Law of Attraction go with your schoolwork, Silas?" Mr. B. asks.

"Well, we'll see, I guess. Every night before I went to sleep, I imagined myself runnin' home from school – excited – can't wait to show my mom my first good grade ever on a paper! I saw her puttin' it on the fridge door, being so proud of me. Even givin' me a big hug and a treat like she did when I was a kid. The more I thought about it, the more I wanted it. I found myself comin' home after school and ole man Henry's store, instead of goin' to the gang house. I even found myself doin' my homework and studyin'!"

"Great, Silas! How do you think you did?"

"Not sure. I'm a little anxious about the test we just took. Can you grade mine now?"

"Sure."

Silas watches nervously as his teacher checks off each answer, hoping each check mark is not a wrong answer. Finally, Mr. Barnes looks up at Silas. His serious look turns into a smile. He marks the paper with an "A" and hands it to the boy. Silas's mouth drops. "Holy cow!" he screams. Then he pumps his power arm, high-fives Mr. B., and runs for home.

"Hey mom – look what I done!" yells Silas as he enters the back door, slamming the screen behind him.

His mother looks over his paper with stunned amazement, then tears.

"Oh, I'm so proud of you, Sugar. I knew you had it in ya. I'm goin' to hang this on the fridge right now." She tapes his paper at eye-level for the whole family to see.

"Let's celebrate," she says. "I'll fix us a treat."

As Silas sits down to eat his milk and cookies, he notices that his teacher has written something else next to his grade. "Thoughts become things ... choose the good ones!" Silas continues to do just that.

~ AFTERWORD ~

What happened to Silas? Did he make it out of the 'hood?

Silas started spending more time working at ole man Henry's Food Mart and less time at the gang house. He felt better about himself when he made money legally. Much safer too. Eventually, Silas made a deal with his gang leader, Madrid, who was quite fond of the boy since Silas took a bullet for him that crazy summer. As payback for his loyalty, Madrid let Silas leave the gang.

With Mr. Barnes's mentorship, Silas started a Law of Attraction study group called *'Hood Vibrations*. Some of the detention gang signed up. Together they learned about visualizing, and about how positive or negative thoughts attract positive or negative people, things, and events into their lives. They learned how to empower their positive thoughts with happy and grateful feelings, as if they had already received what they desired. They took action when inspired by a "gut" feeling.

Silas got better and better at using the Law of Attraction. He and his new friends improved their grades.

Silas and Rudy joined the school basketball team. Other group members joined the Science Club. Some got jobs. *'Hood Vibrations* continued to be a close-knit group all the way through high school.

When it came time for graduation, just as Silas had pictured for years, his mom, sister Latisha, and the twins were in the audience screaming, crying, and waving their arms as he received his diploma from the principal.

Mr. Barnes, seated on the stage with the other teachers, grinned from ear to ear. Most importantly, Silas was proud of himself. He'd done it! And now he was getting out of the 'hood...

I wish to thank my early draft readers for their helpful feedback; my daughter, Inga, for her inner wisdom and teen language suggestions and corrections; my son, Chris, for inspiring the real-life mischievous anecdotes that Silas and Mr. Barnes experienced; my best friend, Kathleen, for her careful editing, encouragement, and belief in this project; and my writing mentor, Sam, without whom I never would have even gotten started! Thank you so much dear ones. And to all the Law of Attraction teachers who have inspired me to change my life in positive ways, I am deeply grateful. Abundant Love and Blessings to you all, ~Ann

SOME YOUTH-ORIENTED RESOURCES:

www.kidsawakening.com,
www.4lifehappykids.com,
www.inspirational-kids-stories.com,
www.LawofAttraction123.com,
www.thewizkids.com,
www.squidoo.com/thesecretforkids,
www.awakeparent.com,
www.ishine.com,
www.EzineArticles.com/?expert=Michael_Losier.

ADDITIONAL LOA RESOURCES:

Rhonda Byrne:	www.thesecret.tv
Mike Dooley:	www.tut.com
Jack Canfield:	www.jackcanfield.com
Esther & Jerry Hicks:	www.abraham-hickslawofattraction.com
Bob Proctor:	www.bobproctor.com
John Assaraf:	www.johnassaraf.com
T. Harv Eker:	www.harveker.com
Lisa Nichols:	www.lisa-nichols.com
Michael Beckwith:	www.Agapelive.com
Bob Doyle:	www.bobdoylesecret.com
Wayne Dyer:	www.drwaynedyer.com
Earl Nightingale:	www.nightingale.com
Louise Hay:	www.LouiseHay.com
Susan Jeffers:	www.susanjeffers.com
Eckhart Tolle:	www.eckharttolle.com
John Randolph Price:	www.johnrandolphprice.com
Michael Beckwith:	www.Agapelive.com
Byron Katie:	www.thework.com
Paul Harrington:	www.thesecretofteenpower.com
Liliane Grace:	www.themasteryclub.com.au